Scrabble Creek

by Patricia Wittmann
illustrated by Nancy Poydar

MACMILLAN PUBLISHING COMPANY   NEW YORK

MAXWELL MACMILLAN CANADA   TORONTO

MAXWELL MACMILLAN INTERNATIONAL

NEW YORK   OXFORD   SINGAPORE   SYDNEY

1 3 5 7 9 10 8 6 4 2

Library of Congress Cataloging-in-Publication Data
Wittmann, Patricia. Scrabble Creek / by Patricia Wittmann ;
illustrated by Nancy Poydar. — 1st ed.   p.   cm. Summary:
A girl camping at Scrabble Creek with her family likes everything about the experience except the nighttime, when she
is afraid of the spooky shadows and strange noises. ISBN
0-02-793225-7 [1. Camping—Fiction. 2. Fear of the dark—
Fiction. 3. Night—Fiction.] I. Poydar, Nancy, ill. II. Title.
PZ7.W818563Sc 1993   [E]—dc20   92-10810

For Cathy, Molly, Steve, Mary, Tom,
Teresa, Paula, and our own Scrabble Creek
—P. W.

To Hank and the mountains
—N. P.

We jump out of the car and run. Down the sand path, over the rocks, and into the shallow water.

"I touched Scrabble Creek!" I shout.

Sam and Steve start splashing. Mom and Alice skip their first rocks.

Plip, plip, plip, plip…plop! All the way across the creek.

Dad lets Baby Lannie's toes touch the water.

I wade out to my favorite rock. The cold water tickles my feet. I sit in the sun with the water bubbling around me. I am Princess Mossy Rock.

I like everything about Scrabble Creek, except….

We carry our stuff up to the bunkhouse. I used to sleep in the little trailer with Mom and Dad, but tonight I am sleeping in the bunkhouse.

I unroll my sleeping bag. It is the oldest and the softest. I am one of the big kids now.

I like everything at Scrabble Creek, except….

"Beat you down to the swimming hole!" Steve shouts. Alice and Sam and I run after him. *Spooosh!* Dad pretends he is a whale.

Swooosh! I swim underwater like an otter and look at everyone's toes.

I like everything about Scrabble Creek, except….

At dinner we eat chicken, potato salad, and corn on the cob. Mmmmm…

"Why does everything taste better here?" I ask.

"So we taste good for the mosquitoes!" says Sam.

I even like Sam's dumb jokes at Scrabble Creek.

Mom puts Baby Lannie to bed in the trailer.

We build a campfire and roast marshmallows.

Frogs begin to croak. *Ka-work, ka-work, ka-work*. I don't listen.

Shadows black as giant crows grow in the trees. I don't look.

"Time for bed, you guys," Mom says.

My flashlight only makes a tiny dot in the dark. The trailer looks small and cosy, but I don't sleep there anymore.

Us big kids walk up together. I hold my breath. I don't think about slugs or mice or foxes or bears.

Snnnap! goes a branch in the woods.

I run up the bunkhouse steps and wiggle to
the very bottom of my sleeping bag. I don't like
the noises. I don't like the blackness.
    I like everything at Scrabble Creek,
except…the night.

But in the morning, the night is gone.

Dad is flipping pancakes. Steve eats the most, ten big ones. After breakfast we play catch on the beach with the leftover pancakes.

I like Scrabble Creek in the morning.

In the afternoon Alice lets me help with the fairy house in the woods. We make moss beds and bark chairs, salmonberry lamps and leaf rugs. Everything a fairy family needs.

I follow Alice to the meadow.

"Shhh!" she says, pointing.

Thistledown fairies float above the grass. They dance in the sunshine.

"They're coming home!" I whisper.

I like Scrabble Creek all day long.

When we leave the meadow, the sun is already beginning to hide.

"Look!" Alice says, jumping up and down, "It's the frog leg!"

I look up and see the big, mossy branch reaching down at me.

"Race you to the picnic table," I say, running off. I don't want to stand under a scary frog leg.

It gets dark before dinner is over. Dad lights the lantern and we play cards in the yellow circle of light.

Ka-work, ka-work. The frogs are already talking.

Wibble, werble, wobble. The creek is loud. I move closer to Dad.

Russsstle, russsstle, crack! The hairs on my neck get prickly. *Thump! Calump!*

"Did you hear that?" I whisper.

"Hear what?" asks Dad, putting his arm around me.

Thump! Calump!

"Oh," says Steve, "just the horse across the creek."

Sam looks into the darkness, "I thought it might be an elephant," he says.

"Elephants don't live here!" I say.

"Then maybe," says Steve, "it's a wild baboon!"

"Or a grrrrrrowling tiger," Mom says deep and low.

"A poodle," says Alice, "Yip-yip, yip-yip!"

"A loon!" Dad says, flapping his arms up and down.

Dad looks silly. He makes me smile.

"Maybe," I whisper, "it's a big, hairy frog."

"Ka-work, ka-work," I croak as deep and loud as I can. All the other animals join in.

We are louder than a zoo. We are louder than a circus. We are louder than the night.

The animals quiet down. It's time to go to bed. Dad picks up the lantern and we walk through the wet grass to the bunkhouse.

Mom tucks me into my sleeping bag.
After they leave, I snuggle down deep. I'm not
so scared now. I am one of the big kids.